Little Mommy

BY SHARON KANE

A GOLDEN BOOK • NEW YORK

This is my house and I am the mommy.
My children are Annabelle, Betsy, and Bonny.

They are good little children and do just as I say.
I put on their coats and they go out to play.

Billy is Daddy; he works in the city.
He has a new car. Isn't it pretty?

I do the dishes and sweep the floor

And wipe the fingerprints off the door.

I wash the clothes in my washing machine.
I scrub them with soap and rinse them clean.

Then I hang them on the line to dry.
I'll have to iron them by and by.

My children like
to go for a ride.
They sit in the buggy
side by side.

Now I will teach you the A B C,
And who can count to ten for me?

I think it's time for me to bake.
I'll make some cookies and ginger cake.

My neighbor comes for a cup of tea.
We have a party by the cherry tree.

Oh, dear! I'm afraid Betsy is ill!
I put her to bed and give her a pill.
I call on the phone for Doctor Dan.
He says he'll come as soon as he can.

Danny is Doctor and he comes in a hurry.
He takes her temperature and says, "Don't worry.
She'll be well as quick as a wink.
It's just the mumbledy bumps, I think."

Dinner is ready, don't be late.
Put on your bibs and sit up straight!
We're having potatoes and blueberry stew.
Now eat your spinach, it's good for you.

Sit on my lap,
   it's story time.
I'll read a poem
   and a nursery rhyme.

It's bath time now for my little dears.
I scrub their necks and wash their ears.

I tuck them in bed
and sing them a song
And they'll be asleep
before very long.

We Mommies have such a lot to do.
Good night, dollies, I'm sleepy too.

® Landoll, Inc.
Ashland, Ohio 44805
© 1995 Coombe Books Ltd.

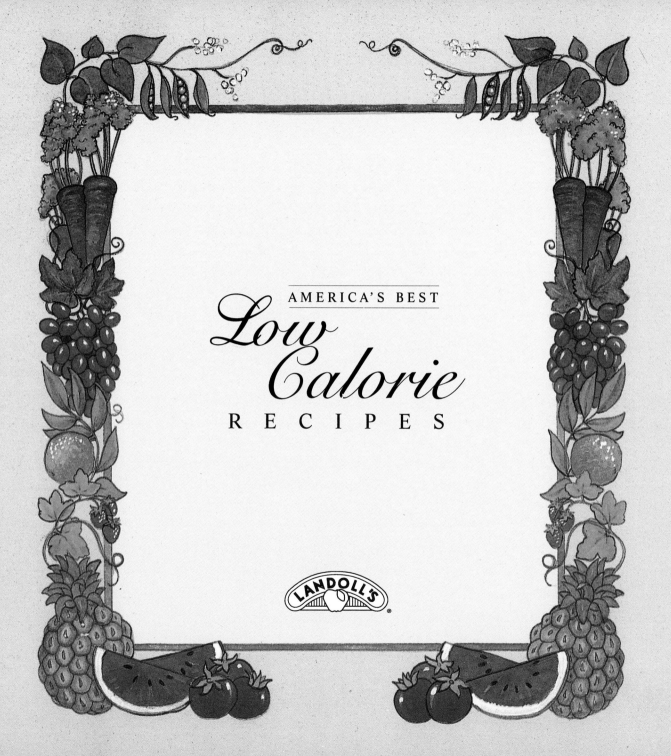

AMERICA'S BEST

Low
Calorie

R E C I P E S

LANDOLL'S

Introduction

$\mathcal{T}$he value of a well-balanced diet in maintaining a healthy weight cannot be overstated. It has long been recognized that being overweight means that you are more susceptible to high blood pressure, thrombosis, and heart attack, and that one of the best ways to improve your general health is to keep a check on your weight.

Many people who want to lose weight quickly over a short period of time opt for a crash diet. Such diets, though they will have an immediate effect, will never be successful in the long term. This is because the body responds to the semi-starvation conditions imposed on it by taking measures to ensure that what reserves there are, are used as economically as possible. The metabolic rate, the rate at which the body uses energy, slows as the body tries to conserve its energy supplies. So, once you begin to eat normally again, you are more likely to gain weight, because the body has become accustomed to storing as much energy as possible, rather than burning it off.

Of the many other, more sensible, ways to lose weight, calorie counting has long been one of the most popular. The food that we eat supplies us with the energy that we need for our bodies to function properly, and calories are a useful unit by which to

measure this energy. In essence, the success of any diet, in terms of weight loss, relies on the principle that less calories should be eaten than used. By knowing the energy value, in terms of calories, of the foods that you eat, it is possible to keep a check on the energy that you are giving your body, enabling you to reach and then to sustain a healthy weight for your height and age.

Obviously, to do this successfully you need to set a realistic target, one that allows the body to function normally. In addition, it is important to use your allotted calorie intake wisely and not to waste it on what are known as "empty" calories, calories that have no nutritional value, containing none of the vitamins, minerals, or fiber needed by the body. Refined sugar is a particular offender, and it is for this reason that it is important to try to stay away from cookies and cakes. Frequently, processed foods also contain large amounts of sugar and it is always wise to check the labels before buying.

These delicious recipes are designed to be included in a pattern of healthy eating that is both low in calories and high in enjoyment. They show that a low calorie diet need not be limited in its scope, and delicious, full-flavored meals do not have to be fattening. In addition, all the recipes are calorie counted, enabling you to plan your menu quickly and easily.

Melon and Prosciutto

SERVES 4

This typically Italian dish makes a light appetizer and is wonderful served on hot summer days.

PREPARATION: 15 mins
115 CALORIES PER SERVING

1 large ripe melon, Cassaba or Crenshaw
16 thin slices prosciutto ham
French flat leaf parsley to garnish

1. Cut the melon in half lengthwise. Using a spoon, scoop out and discard all the seeds and fibers.

Step 1 Using a spoon, scoop out and discard the seeds and fibrous core of the melon.

Note; Prosciutto is raw ham, and is not always available in the U.S. If you cannot get it, use very thinly sliced Smithfield ham.

Step 4 Roll a slice of prosciutto ham around each thin slice of melon.

2. Cut the melon into quarters and carefully peel away the skin using a sharp knife.

3. Cut each quarter into 4 thin slices.

4. Wrap each slice of melon in a slice of the prosciutto ham, and arrange on a serving platter. Chill well and garnish with parsley before serving.

Spicy Tomato Soup

SERVES 4

This highly fragrant and spicy tomato soup makes an interesting low calorie appetizer.

PREPARATION: 15 mins
COOKING: 17-18 mins
41 CALORIES PER SERVING

---

3 medium tomatoes
1 medium onion, finely chopped
2 tbsps oil
1 green chili pepper, seeded and chopped
3 cloves garlic, crushed
1 tbsp tomato paste
1 quart water, or vegetable broth
4-6 green curry leaves, or ½ tsp curry powder
Salt
Coriander (cilantro) leaves and green
    chilies for garnish

---

1. Cut a small cross in the skin of each tomato and steep in boiling water 30-40 seconds.

Step 2 Remove the tomatoes from the boiling water and carefully peel away the loosened skin.

Step 3 Cut away and discard the hard green core from the tomatoes, and chop the flesh roughly with a sharp knife.

2. Remove the tomatoes and carefully peel away the loosened skin with a sharp knife.

3. Remove the core from the tomatoes and roughly chop the flesh.

4. Heat the oil in a large saucepan and gently sauté the onion, chopped chili and garlic for 3-4 minutes until it is soft, but not browned.

5. Stir in the chopped tomatoes and cook 5 minutes, stirring often.

6. Blend the tomato paste with the water and pour this into the onions and tomatoes. Add the curry leaves or powder, season with the salt and simmer 5-7 minutes.

7. Remove the soup from the heat and stir in the coriander leaves and the chili halves.

8. Serve piping hot, discarding the chili garnish before eating.

Carrot Soup

SERVES 4
This warming, tasty soup is filling yet low in calories

PREPARATION: 12 mins
COOKING: 25-30 mins
44 CALORIES PER SERVING

1 pound carrots
1 medium onion
1 turnip
2 cloves garlic, crushed
1 quart water or vegetable broth
½ tsp dried thyme
½ tsp ground nutmeg
Salt and pepper, to taste
Toasted sunflower seeds, flaked almonds and
   pistachio nuts, mixed together for garnish

1. Peel the carrots and cut them into thick slices.

To chop an onion finely, pierce the peeled onion with a fork and use this to hold the vegetable steady whilst you chop.

Step 6 Purée the soup until it is creamy and smooth.

2. Peel and roughly chop the onion and turnip.

3. Put the vegetables, garlic, and water or broth, into a large saucepan and bring to the boil. Cover the pan, reduce the heat and simmer 20 minutes.

4. Add all the seasonings and simmer a further 5 minutes.

5. Remove the soup from the heat and allow to cool.

6. Using a liquidizer, blend the soup until it is thick and smooth.

7. Reheat the soup, garnishing with the seeds and nuts before serving.

Fresh Tomato Omelet

SERVES 2

Omelets can make substantial low calorie lunches or light meals.

PREPARATION: 25 mins
COOKING: 5 mins
252 CALORIES PER SERVING

1 pound fresh tomatoes
Salt and pepper
4 eggs
4 tbsps water
½ tsp fresh chopped basil
2 tbsps olive or vegetable oil
½ tsp fresh chopped oregano or basil to
   garnish

1. Cut a small cross into the skins of each tomato and plunge them into boiling water. Leave 30 seconds, then remove them with a slotted spoon.

2. Using a sharp knife, carefully peel away the tomato skins and discard them.

Step 3 Remove the seeds and juice from the halved tomatoes with a teaspoon.

Step 5 Whisk the eggs, water and herbs together thoroughly, until they are frothy.

3. Cut the tomatoes in half and remove and discard the seeds, juice, and any tough core.

4. Cut the tomato flesh into thin strips.

5. Break the eggs into a bowl and whisk in the water and chopped herbs. Season with salt and pepper and continue whisking until the egg mixture is frothy.

6. Heat the oil in a large skillet, then pour in the egg mixture.

7. Using a spatula, stir the egg mixture around the pan about 2-3 minutes, or until the eggs are beginning to set.

8. Spread the tomato strips over the partially-cooked eggs, and continue cooking without stirring until the eggs have completely set and the tomatoes are just warmed through.

9. Sprinkle with the additional chopped basi¹ before serving.

Vegetable Kebobs

SERVES 4

A delicious way to serve fresh vegetables as part of a low calorie diet.

PREPARATION: 30 mins, plus time to marinate vegetables

COOKING: 10 mins

83 CALORIES PER SERVING

---

1 large eggplant
Salt
1 large green bell pepper
4 zucchini
12-14 cherry tomatoes
12-14 pearl onions
12-14 button mushrooms
4 tbsps olive oil
2 tbsps lemon juice
½ tsp salt
½ tsp freshly ground black pepper

---

1. Cut the eggplant in half and dice it into 1-inch pieces.

2. Put the eggplant pieces into a large bowl, and sprinkle liberally with salt. Stir well and allow to stand 30 minutes to draw out the bitter juices.

3. Rinse the eggplant pieces thoroughly in a colander under cold water.

4. Cut the bell pepper in half. Remove and discard the core and seeds and cut the pepper

Step 8 Thread the prepared and marinated vegetables alternately onto kebob skewers.

flesh into 1-inch pieces with a sharp knife.

5. Slice the zucchini diagonally into 1-inch pieces.

6. Remove the tough cores from the cherry tomatoes and peel the onions. Rinse the mushrooms under cold water, but do not peel.

7. Put all the prepared vegetables into a large bowl and pour in the remaining ingredients. Mix well to coat evenly, cover and allow to stand about 30 minutes, stirring once or twice.

8. Thread the vegetables alternately onto skewers and arrange them on a broiler pan.

9. Brush the kebobs with the marinade and broil 3-4 minutes, turning frequently and basting with the marinade until they are evenly browned. Serve piping hot.

Ratatouille

SERVES 6

A classic vegetable casserole from the south of France.

PREPARATION: 20 mins, plus 30 mins standing time
COOKING: 35 mins
84 CALORIES PER SERVING

---

2 eggplants
Salt
4 zucchini
4 tbsps olive oil
2 Bermuda (red) onions
2 green or red bell peppers
2 tsps chopped fresh basil
1 large clove garlic, crushed
1 pound 12 ounces canned plum tomatoes
Salt and freshly ground black pepper
⅔ cup dry white wine

---

1. Cut the eggplants in half lengthwise and score each cut surface diagonally, using the point of a sharp knife.

Step 8 Gently fry the chopped eggplant in the vegetable juices and oil, until they begin to brown.

2. Sprinkle the eggplants liberally with salt and allow to stand 30 minutes. After this time, rinse them thoroughly and pat them dry.

3. Roughly chop the eggplants and slice the zucchini thickly. Set them to one side.

4. Peel the onions and half them. Cut them into thin slices with a sharp knife.

5. Cut the bell peppers in half lengthwise and remove and discard the seeds and white parts. Chop the flesh roughly.

6. Heat the oil in a large saucepan, and sauté the onion slices for 5 minutes until they are soft.

7. Stir in the peppers and zucchini, and cook gently 5 minutes until they begin to soften. Remove all the vegetables from the pan and set aside.

8. Put the chopped eggplants into the saucepan with the vegetable juices. Cook gently until the mixture begins to brown, then add all the other ingredients to the pan.

9. Add the canned tomatoes, garlic, and basil to the saucepan along with the sautéed vegetables, mixing well. Bring to the boil, then reduce the heat and simmer 15 minutes.

10. Add the wine to the pan and continue cooking for a further 15 minutes before serving.

Casserole of Veal and Mushrooms

SERVES 6

*Veal is a low-fat meat and is delicious when served in this tomato
and mushroom sauce.*

PREPARATION: 30 mins
COOKING: 1hr 30 mins
275 CALORIES PER SERVING

3 pounds lean veal
Salt and pepper
4 tbsps olive oil
2 shallots, finely chopped
½ clove garlic, peeled and crushed
6 tbsps dry white wine
1¼ cups strong beef broth or consommé
1 cup canned tomatoes, drained and chopped
1 bouquet garni (parsley, bayleaf, chervil and
    thyme)
2 strips lemon peel
½ cup button mushrooms
2 tbsps fresh chopped parsley

1. Dice the meat into bite-size pieces, using a
sharp knife.

2. Sprinkle the pieces of meat with salt and
pepper, then allow to stand about 30 minutes.

3. Heat half of the oil in a large skillet, and
sauté the pieces of meat 5-10 minutes, stirring
frequently. Remove the meat from the pan and
set it aside.

4. Add the shallots and garlic to the oil and

Step 4 Cook
the garlic and
shallots in the
hot oil and
meat juices
gently, taking
care to soften
but not brown
them.

meat juices in the pan, lower the heat and cook
until softened. Return the veal to the pan and
mix well.

5. Add the wine, broth, tomatoes, bouquet
garni, and lemon peel to the meat mixture, and
bring to the boil.

6. Transfer the veal to an ovenproof casserole.
Cover with a tight-fitting lid and bake in a pre-
heated 325°F oven about 1¼ hours, or until the
meat is tender.

7. Heat the remaining oil in a clean skillet, and
cook the mushrooms 2-3 minutes.

8. When the meat in the casserole is tender, stir
in the mushrooms and continue cooking in the
oven a further 15 minutes.

9. Sprinkle with the chopped parsley before
serving.

Chicken Escalopes

SERVES 4

Although the chicken is sautéed in oil, it is only enough to brown the meat without adding too many calories.

PREPARATION: 20 mins
COOKING: 10-15 mins
300 CALORIES PER SERVING

---

4 chicken breasts, boned and skinned
1 egg white
8 tbsps wholewheat breadcrumbs
1 tbsp chopped fresh sage
Salt and pepper
2 tbsps walnut oil
½ cup low-calorie mayonnaise
⅔ cup plain yogurt
1 tsp grated fresh horseradish
2 tbsps chopped walnuts
Lemon slices and chopped walnuts to garnish

---

1. Pat the chicken breasts dry with kitchen paper.

2. Whisk the egg whites with a fork until they just begin to froth, but are still liquid.

3. Carefully brush all surfaces of the chicken breasts with the beaten egg white.

4. Put the breadcrumbs onto a shallow plate and stir in the chopped sage. Season with a little salt and pepper.

5. Place the chicken breasts, one at a time, onto the plate of breadcrumbs and sage, and

Step 5 Press the bread-crumb-and-sage mixture onto the chicken breasts.

carefully press this mixture onto the surfaces of the chicken.

6. Put the oil into a large shallow skillet, and gently sauté the chicken 5 minutes on each side. Test that the meat is cooked by piercing with a skewer. If the juices do not run clear, sautée a few minutes more. Set aside, and keep warm.

7. Mix all the remaining ingredients except for the garnish in a small bowl, whisking well to blend the yogurt and mayonnaise evenly.

8. Place the cooked chicken breasts on a serving platter, and spoon a little of the sauce over. Serve garnished with the lemon slices and additional chopped nuts.

Paprika Schnitzel

SERVES 4

Peppers, paprika, and wine give a hearty flavor to this easily-prepared dish.

Preparation: 30 mins
Cooking: approximately 20 mins
230 calories per serving

---

8 thin slices pork fillet, sliced lengthwise
Salt and pepper
1 garlic clove, crushed
3 tbsps vegetable oil
1 medium onion
1 red bell pepper
1 green bell pepper
1 tbsp paprika
⅔ cup beef broth
½ cup red wine
3 tbsps tomato paste
⅔ cup plain low fat yogurt

---

1. Trim the slices of pork to remove any fat, and flatten them out with a rolling pin until they are ¼-inch thick.

2. Rub both sides of the pork fillets with salt, pepper, and garlic, then allow to stand in a refrigerator for 30 minutes.

3. Heat the oil in a large skillet, and cook the pork fillets until they are well browned and cooked right through, approximately 4 minutes on each side.

4. Remove the pork from the pan, set aside, and keep warm.

Step 1 Flatten the pork fillets out with a rolling pin until they are ¼-inch thick.

5. Peel the onion and thinly slice it into rings. Cut the peppers in half and remove and discard the seeds and white parts. Slice the peppers lengthwise into thin strips.

6. Add the onion rings and the sliced peppers to the oil and meat juices in the skillet, and cook quickly about 3-4 minutes until they are soft.

7. Add the paprika, broth, wine, and tomato paste to the skillet and bring the mixture to the boil.

8. Reduce the heat and simmer until the liquid has evaporated and the sauce has thickened. Season to taste.

9. Arrange the pork slices on a serving platter, and pour the paprika sauce over the top of them.

10. Beat the yogurt in a bowl until it is smooth, then carefully drizzle it over the paprika sauce to make an attractive pattern. Serve hot.

Kidneys with Mustard Sauce

SERVES 4

Lambs' kidneys have a delicate flavor, which a mustard sauce complements perfectly.

PREPARATION: 25 mins
COOKING: 15 mins
220 CALORIES PER SERVING

---

4 tbsps vegetable oil
1½ pounds lambs' kidneys
1-2 shallots, peeled and finely chopped
1¼ cups dry white wine
3 tbsps Dijon-style mustard
Salt, pepper and lemon juice, to taste
2 tbsps fresh chopped parsley

---

1. Cut the kidneys in half lengthwise, and carefully snip out the core and tough tubes.

2. Heat the oil in a large skillet, and gently sauté the kidneys about 10 minutes, stirring them frequently until they are light brown on all sides. Remove the kidneys from the pan and keep them warm.

Step 1 Trim any fat or tubes away from the core of each kidney, using a sharp knife or small pair of scissors.

Step 2 Sauté the kidneys in the hot oil, stirring them frequently to brown evenly on all sides.

3. Add the shallots to the pan and cook about 1 minute, stirring frequently until they soften.

4. Add the wine and bring to the boil, stirring constantly and scraping the pan to remove any brown juices.

5. Allow the wine to boil rapidly 3-4 minutes, until it has reduced by about half. Remove the pan from the heat.

6. Using a balloon whisk or fork, mix the mustard into the reduced wine along with salt, pepper, lemon juice to taste, and half of the fresh chopped parsley.

7. Return the kidneys to the pan and cook over a low heat 1-2 minutes, stirring all the time to heat the kidneys through evenly. Serve immediately, sprinkled with the remaining parsley.

Broiled Whole Fish

SERVES 4

Broiling fish with herbs and lemon is a delicious, healthy way to cook fish.

PREPARATION: 20 mins
COOKING: 16-20 mins, depending upon the size
    of the fish
APPROX. 180 CALORIES PER SERVING

2 large bream, porgy or other whole fish
Fresh thyme and oregano
Olive oil
Lemon juice
Salt and pepper
Lemon wedges

Step 1 To make lemon wedges cut the ends off the lemons, then cut in 4 or 8 wedges.

1. Preheat a broiler. Gut the fish and rinse it well. Pat dry and sprinkle the cavity with salt, pepper, and lemon juice. Place sprigs of herbs inside.

2. Make 3 diagonal cuts on the sides of the fish with a sharp knife. Place the fish on the broiler rack and sprinkle with olive oil and lemon juice.

3. Cook on both sides until golden brown and crisp. This should take about 8-10 minutes per side, depending on the thickness of the fish.

4. Serve the fish on a large platter surrounded with lemon wedges.

Step 2 Use a sharp knife to make diagonal cuts on both sides of each fish.

Sole Kebobs

SERVES 4

*Fish is highly nutritious, easy to cook, and makes an ideal contribution
to a healthy diet.*

PREPARATION: 30 mins, plus marinating time
COOKING: 8 mins
254 CALORIES PER SERVING

---

8 fillets of sole
4 tbsps olive oil
1 clove garlic, peeled and crushed
Juice ½ lemon
Finely grated rind ½ lemon
Salt and pepper
3 drops of Tabasco sauce
3 zucchini
1 green bell pepper
Freshly chopped parsley for garnish

---

1. Using a sharp knife, carefully peel the skin from the backs of each sole fillet.

2. Cut each sole fillet in half lengthwise, and roll each slice up like a jellyroll.

3. Mix together the oil, garlic, lemon juice,

Step 1 Use a sharp knife to cut between the meat of the fish and the skin. Lift the meat up and away as you cut.

Step 7 Thread the marinated rolls of fish onto kebob skewers, alternating these with vegetables.

rind, and seasonings in a small bowl.

4. Put the rolls of fish into a shallow dish and pour over the marinade. Cover and allow to stand in a cool place for at least 2 hours.

5. Cut the zucchini into ¼-inch slices.

6. Cut the peppers in half lengthwise and remove the white core and the seeds. Chop the pepper flesh into 1-inch squares.

7. Carefully thread the marinated sole fillets onto kebob skewers, alternating these with pieces of the prepared vegetables. Brush each kebob with a little of the marinade.

8. Arrange the kebobs on a broiler pan and cook under a moderately hot broiler for about 8 minutes, turning frequently, and brushing with the extra marinade to keep them moist.

9. Arrange the kebobs on a serving platter, and sprinkle with the chopped parsley.

Watercress and Orange Salad

SERVES 4-6

This colorful salad looks best when served on a bed of grated carrot.

PREPARATION: 20 mins

200 CALORIES PER SERVING

3 large bunches of watercress
4 oranges
6 tbsps oil
Juice and rind of 1 orange
Pinch sugar
1 tsp lemon juice
Salt and pepper

1. Wash the watercress and carefully cut away any thick stalks. Break the watercress into small sprigs, discarding any yellow leaves.

Step 2 Carefully peel the oranges using a sharp knife, and collecting any juices in a small bowl.

Step 3 Cut the orange segments carefully from between the inner membranes using a sharp knife.

2. Carefully remove the peel and white parts from the oranges using a sharp knife. Catch any juice that spills in a small bowl.

3. Cut carefully, remove the fleshy segments from between the thin membrane inside the orange.

4. Arrange the watercress with the orange segments on a serving platter.

5. Put the remaining ingredients into the bowl with the reserved orange juice, and mix together well.

6. Pour the salad dressing over the oranges and watercress just before serving, to prevent the watercress from going limp.

Tuna, Bean and Tomato Salad

SERVES 6

This salad is a meal in itself, containing a good balance of protein and fiber.

PREPARATION: 25 mins, plus overnight soaking
180 CALORIES PER SERVING

---

1 cup dried flageolet beans
¾ canned tuna in brine
Juice of 1 lemon
½ cup olive oil
1 tsp chopped parsley, basil or marjoram
Salt and pepper
8 firm tomatoes

---

1. Put the beans into a bowl and pour over enough cold water to just cover. Allow to soak overnight.

2. Drain the beans and put them into a sauce-pan. Cover with boiling water, then simmer at least 1 hour. Drain thoroughly and cool.

3. Drain the can of tuna and flake it into a bowl.

Step 5 Mix the dressing into the salad by tossing it carefully, to ensure that the tuna does not break up too much.

Step 8 When blanched, the skins on the tomatoes should peel away very easily if you use a sharp knife.

4. Put the lemon juice, olive oil, herbs, and seasoning into a small bowl and whisk together with a fork.

5. Stir the beans into the tuna fish and mix in the dressing, tossing the salad together carefully so that the dressing is thoroughly incorporated.

6. Adjust the seasoning and arrange the salad in a mound on a shallow serving platter.

7. Cut a small cross into the skins of the tomato and plunge them into boiling water for 30 seconds.

8. Using a sharp knife, carefully peel away the skins from the tomatoes.

9. Slice the tomatoes thinly and arrange them around the edge of the bean and tuna salad. Serve immediately.

Stir-fried Salad

SERVES 4

Stir-fries are served hot, but the ingredients are cooked so quickly that they retain all of their crunchiness.

PREPARATION: 15 mins
COOKING: 10 mins
99 CALORIES PER SERVING

1 onion
2 large leeks
4 tbsps olive oil
2 cloves garlic, crushed
8 ounces snowpeas, topped and tailed
½ cup beansprouts or alfalfa sprouts
Salt and pepper
1 tbsp fresh chopped coriander (cilantro)
   leaves

1. Peel the onion and cut it into thin rings.

Step 2 Rinse the split leek under running water, separating the leaves to wash out any dirt.

Step 3 Cut the pieces of leek lengthwise into thin strips.

2. Trim the leeks and cut down the length of one side. Open the leek out and wash it thoroughly under running water.

3. Cut the leek into 3 pieces, then thinly slice each piece lengthwise into thin strips.

4. Heat the oil in a large skillet, and add the onions and garlic. Cook 2 minutes, stirring all the time until the onions have softened but not browned.

5. Add the snow peas and sliced leeks to the wok and continue stir-frying 4 minutes.

6. Add the remaining ingredients and cook briskly a further 2 minutes. Serve piping hot.

Sunburst Figs

SERVES 4

Fresh figs can make an attractive dessert and have the added benefit of being very low in calories.

PREPARATION: 15 mins plus chiling time
101 CALORIES PER SERVING

---

4 fresh figs
½ cup cranberries or other red berry
6 oranges
1 tsp orange-flower water

---

1. Trim the stalks away from the top of the figs, but do not peel them.

2. Cut the figs into quarters lengthwise, taking care not to sever them completely at the base.

3. Press the fig quarters open gently with your fingers, to make a flower shape. Place each fig carefully on a serving platter.

4. Arrange a few berries carefully on the center of each fig.

Step 2 Cut the figs into quarters lengthwise with a sharp knife, without cutting through the base completely.

Step 3 Carefully press open the quarters of each fig to make an attractive flower shape.

5. Cut 2 of the oranges in half, and squeeze out the juice. Mix this juice with the orange-flower water in a small jug.

6. Carefully cut away the peel and white parts from the remaining 4 oranges.

7. Using a sharp knife, cut the segments of orange away from the inside of the thin membranes, keeping each piece intact as a crescent shape.

8. Arrange the orange segments in between the petals of the fig flower on the serving platter.

9. Spoon equal amounts of the orange sauce over each fig, and chill thoroughly before serving.

Strawberry Yogurt Ice

SERVES 4

*Ice cream is usually forbidden on a low calorie diet, but when prepared with low fat
plain yogurt and fresh fruit, it can provide a welcome treat.*

PREPARATION: 15 mins plus freezing time
63 CALORIES PER SERVING

8 ounces fresh strawberries
1¼ cups low fat plain yogurt
2 tsps powdered gelatin
2 tbsps boiling water
1 egg white
Sweetener to taste

1. Remove and discard the green stalks and leaves from the top of the strawberries. Roughly chop the fruit.

2. Place the strawberries into a liquidizer along with the yogurt. Blend until smooth.

3. Sprinkle the gelatin over the boiling water in a small bowl. Stand the bowl in another, and pour in enough boiling water to come halfway up the sides of the dish.

4. Allow the gelatin to stand, without stirring, until it has dissolved and the liquid has cleared.

5. Pour the strawberry mixture into a bowl, and stir in the dissolved gelatin, mixing well. Place the bowl in the freezer and chill until just icy around the edges.

Step 2 Blend the strawberries and yogurt together until they are smooth.

6. Remove the bowl from the freezer and beat until the chilled mixture is smooth. Return the bowl to the freezer and freeze once again in the same way.

7. Remove the bowl from the freezer a second time, and whisk until smooth. Whisk the egg white until it forms soft peaks.

8. Fold the whisked egg white into the partially set strawberry mixture, carefully lifting and cutting the mixture to keep it light.

9. Sweeten with the sweetener to taste, then pour the strawberry ice into a shallow-sided ice cream dish, and return to the freezer to freeze until completely set.

10. Remove the ice cream 10 minutes before serving to soften slightly.

Exotic Fruit Salad

SERVES 4-6

Mangoes are exceptionally sweet when ripe, and give this lovely fruit salad a natural tangy sweetness.

PREPARATION: 25 mins, plus 1 hr chiling time
100 CALORIES PER SERVING

---

3 ripe peaches
3 kiwi fruits
1 large starfruit (carambola)
½ cup fresh strawberries
2 well-ripened mangoes, each weighing about
 12 ounces
Juice of half a lime
½ cup redcurrants or blueberries

---

1. Plunge the peaches into boiling water for a few seconds, then carefully peel away the skin.

2. Carefully cut the peaches in half and pit them.

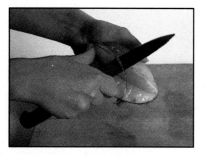

Step 5 Cut away any brown pieces from the skin of the star fruit using a sharp knife.

3. Cut the peach halves into thin slices and arrange on a serving platter.

4. Cut away the peel from the kiwi fruits and slice them.

5. Trim away any dark pieces from the skin of the starfruit, cut the flesh into thin slices, and remove any small seeds you may find.

6. Leave the green stems on the strawberries and cut them in half lengthwise. Arrange all the prepared fruit on the serving platter with the peaches.

7. Peel the mango and chop away the flesh from the large inner stone.

8. Put the chopped mango flesh into a liquidizer, along with the lime juice and half of the berries.

9. Purée the mixture until smooth, then press the pulp through a sieve to remove the skins and seeds.

10. Sprinkle the remaining berries over the fruit on the serving platter, removing any hard stems or leaves as you do so.

11. Pour the fruit purée evenly over the fruit salad, and chill at least 1 hour before serving.

Index

Sunburst Figs make an ideal low calorie dessert.